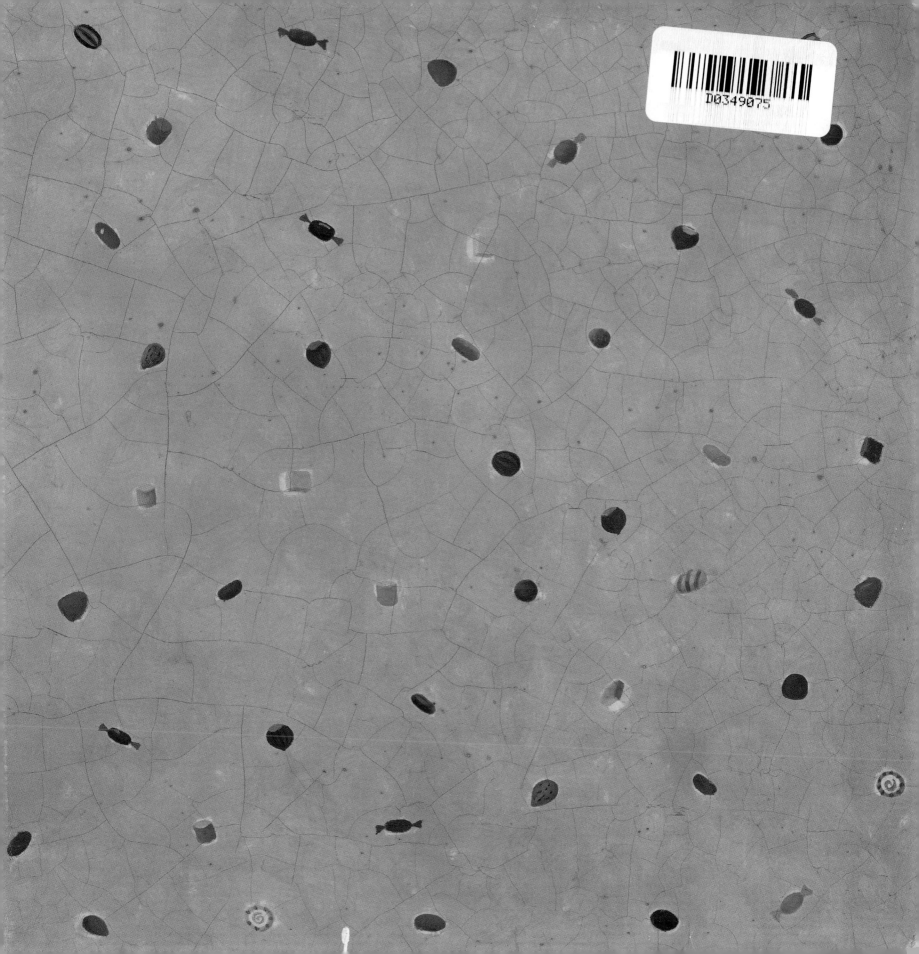

The Nutcracker

illustrations by Alison Jay

templar publishing

For Eleanor Esmae –

happy first birthday. Love from Alison x

A TEMPLAR BOOK

First published in the UK in 2011 by Templar Publishing,
an imprint of The Templar Company Limited,
The Granary, North Street, Dorking, Surrey, RH4 1DN, UK
www.templarco.co.uk

Text copyright © 2010 by Penguin Group (USA) Inc.
Illustrations copyright © 2010 by Alison Jay

Based on the story by E. T. A. Hoffman
Retold by AnnMarie Anderson

Originally published in the United States in 2010 by Dial Books for Young Readers,
a division of Penguin Young Readers Group,
345 Hudson Street, New York, New York 10014, U.S.A.
www.penguin.com/youngreaders

First edition

ISBN 978-1-84877-017-1

Printed in China

It was Christmas Eve and little Clara, watching the snow fall outside,
could hardly wait for Godfather Drosselmeyer to arrive for the party.

As if on cue, the door burst open. There was Godfather Drosselmeyer, with his flowing cape and curly moustache. "Merry Christmas!" he bellowed.

Godfather Drosselmeyer was a famous toy maker, so the children immediately gathered round as he reached under his cape and produced one bright package after another.

Clara's younger
brother Fritz got a wooden
toy sword. Her cousin Anne got
a lovely doll with sparkling fairy wings.
And Ben, the youngest cousin, got a wind-
up mouse that was so fuzzy and grey it almost
looked real.

But Clara knew her present was the best of all. It was a
toy soldier, and if you put a nut between its teeth and pulled the
lever in its back, it cracked the shell right open.

"Oh, thank you Godfather," breathed Clara.

Clara passed the Nutcracker around for everyone to try. But Fritz shoved a huge walnut between its teeth. When he pulled the lever down hard the Nutcracker's jaw snapped!

"Do not worry, Clara," said Godfather Drosselmeyer pulling out a handkerchief and tying it around the Nutcracker's head. "That should do for now. Tomorrow, I'll get my tools and fix him properly."

Clara gave the Nutcracker a kiss and placed him gently under the Christmas tree with all of the other toys. Then, reluctantly, she went upstairs to bed.

But try as she might, Clara couldn't sleep. Late that night, she tiptoed back downstairs and curled up beneath the tree, with the Nutcracker snug in her arms. Finally, she drifted off.

Clara woke with a start as the grandfather clock chimed loudly.
She glanced around and rubbed her eyes. Something incredible was
happening. The Christmas tree and the toys appeared to be growing!
Soon, Clara was standing face-to-face with the Nutcracker.

Suddenly, an army of mice marched towards Clara from behind the sofa, led by a very large, very fuzzy grey mouse with a golden crown. The Nutcracker pulled a wooden sword from his side and marched forward, leading the toys into battle to protect Clara.

But his wooden sword was no match for
the Mouse King's shiny metal one. Clara had to
do something. She tore her slipper from her foot
and threw it at the Mouse King with all her might.

The Mouse King crumpled to the ground, his crown
spinning to rest beside him.

Clara couldn't believe her eyes – as the Mouse King
fell, the Nutcracker magically transformed into a Prince.

Sweeping the Mouse King's crown from the floor, he placed it on Clara's head. "Thank you," he said. "I've been trapped in the shape of the Nutcracker for many years. But your bravery broke the Mouse King's spell. Now I am free."

Speechless, Clara looked down to see that her nightdress had turned into a magnificent gown.

The Prince held out his hand. "Would you come to my kingdom, the Land of Sweets?"

"Oh, how lovely!" said Clara, and together they sped off in a grand sleigh.

As the sleigh raced across the Land of Snow, the stars sparkled like diamonds in the sky and dazzling snowflakes danced all around them.

Before long, the sleigh pulled up to a marvellous castle with candyfloss
trees and sugar cane gates. Clara blinked in disbelief.
"This is where I live – the Marzipan Palace," said the Prince. A beautiful girl
had appeared beside him. "And this is the Sugar Plum Fairy."

"Welcome to the Land of Sweets," said the Sugar Plum Fairy to Clara, smiling warmly. The Prince explained how Clara had saved his life by bravely defeating the Mouse King. "We must have a a great banquet in your honour!" the Sugar Plum Fairy declared.

As the guests sat down, waiters
wheeled out a giant box of chocolates.

Suddenly, two Spanish dancers
leaped out, clicking their castanets.

Then, a giant teapot, cup and saucer were pushed into the room. Three graceful Chinese acrobats sprang from the teapot and whirled dramatically across the floor.

Next, four Arabian dancers leaped out of the teacup, followed by a troupe of Russian performers, who crossed the room in a dazzling series of jumps and kicks.

After a short pause, Mother Ginger emerged, wearing an enormous skirt.

Clara giggled in surprise as six French children scampered out from beneath it, spinning like candy-coloured tops around the room.

Finally, the Sugar Plum Fairy and the Prince danced a magnificent duet. Clara was breathless from clapping and cheering.

Each time the Sugar Plum Fairy spun around, her sparkling skirt and wings reflected specks of moonlight around the room.

As the festivities wound down, Clara stifled a yawn.
"It is time we took you home," the Prince told her softly.
Placing Clara gently inside the sleigh, he whispered something in the horse's ear. In an instant the sleigh was whisking Clara back through the snow.

On Christmas morning, Clara woke in her own cosy bed. Her beautiful gown had turned back into a nightdress, and when she reached up for her crown, there was nothing there.

Then Clara noticed a flash of red beside her. It was her Nutcracker – without the handkerchief bandage and perfectly whole! Clara hugged him close. Though she never told a soul about her adventure, she hoped in her heart that every Christmas Eve might be as magical as this one.

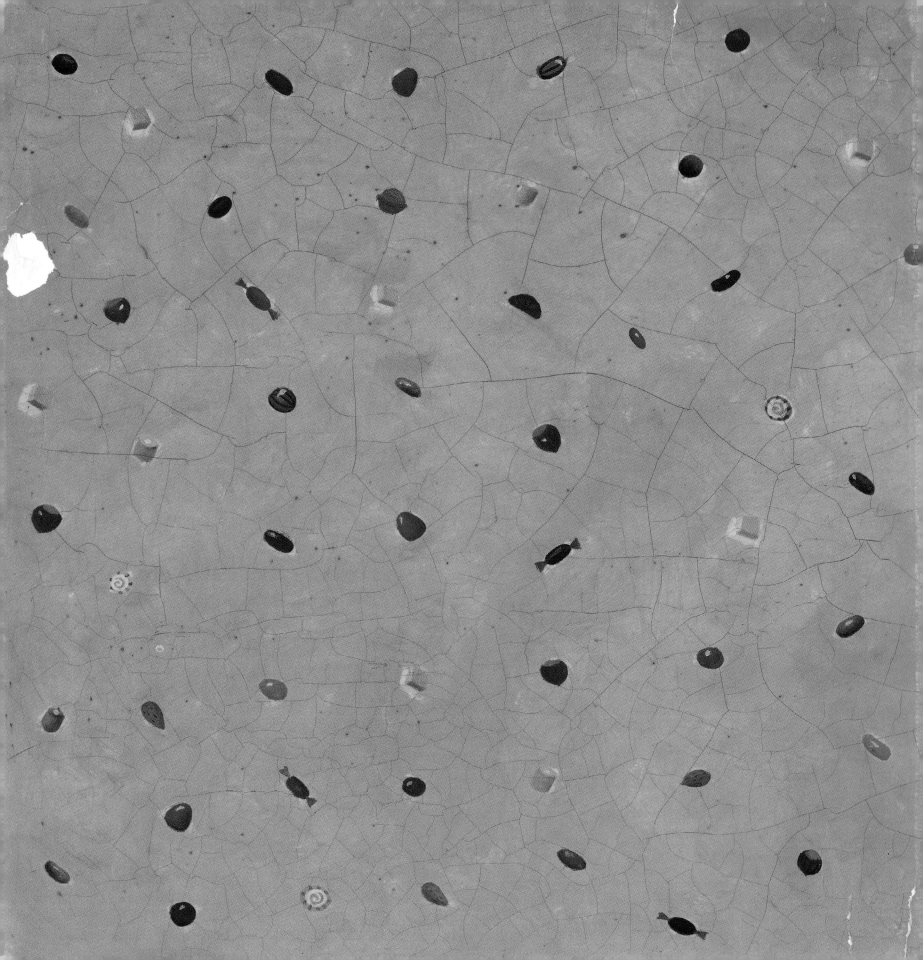